*Samuel French Acting Edition*

CW00557048

# Hammered

# A Thor & Loki Play

## *by* Christian Borle

Based on the Marvel Comics *by* Stan Lee, Larry Lieber & Jack Kirby

## FOR PRODUCTION ENQUIRIES

UNITED STATES AND CANADA
info@concordtheatricals.com
1-866-979-0447

UNITED KINGDOM AND EUROPE
licensing@concordtheatricals.co.uk
020-7054-7200

Each title is subject to availability from Concord Theatricals Corp.,
depending upon country of performance. Please be aware that
*HAMMERED* may not be licensed by Concord Theatricals Corp. in
your territory. Professional and amateur producers should contact the
nearest Concord Theatricals Corp. office or licensing partner to verify
availability.

Please refer to page 50 for further copyright information.

## FOR MARVEL ENTERTAINMENT, INC.

Dan Buckley – President

Joe Quesada – Chief Creative Officer

Alan Fine – Executive Producer

Stephen Wacker – VP, Creative & Content Development

Sana Amanat – VP, Content & Character Development

Nick Lowe – Executive Editor, Vice President for Content, Digital
    Publishing

John Nee – Publisher

Mike Pasciullo – Senior Vice President, Global Marketing &
    Communications

Mitch Montgomery – Executive Director, Brand & Creative Operations

## SPECIAL THANKS

CB Cebulski, David Bogart, Tim Cheng, Ashley Irving, Rickey Purdin,
Ellie Pyle, Darren Sanchez

## ADDITIONAL CREDITS

### Dramaturg

Ken Cerniglia

### Contributors

Matt Hagmeier Curtis, Julie Haverkate, Pearl Hodiwala, Sarah Kenny,
Janette Martinez, Lisa Mitchell, David Redman Scott, Dorman High
School (Roebuck, SC), Floyd Central High School (Floyds Knobbs, IN),
Kamehameha School (Honolulu, HI), Los Angeles County High School
for the Arts (Los Angeles, CA), New World School of the Arts (Miami,
FL), Riverton High School (Riverton, UT), Saint Ignatius High School
(Cleveland, OH), Staples High School (Westport, CT)

# MARVEL SPOTLIGHT

Welcome, True Believers!

I'm so glad to have you join us and take your place amongst the legendary pantheon of Marvel heroes.

In the early 1960s, Marvel was a small, upstart comic book company introducing little-known characters like Spider-Man, The Avengers, Black Panther, and so many more that are household names today. It's been an exciting ride over the last 20 years as we've expanded from the printed page to animation, television, movies, and games. Complete and total world domination... well, almost. I've been fortunate enough to serve at Marvel during this time, first as Editor-in-Chief and now as Chief Creative Officer, and I firmly believe that our success in each of these mediums has come from our love for the characters and an unbridled excitement that we bring to each new challenge. That's why I can't begin to tell you how thrilled I am about Marvel Spotlight and your participation in it – it's going to be amazing to see you bring these stories to life.

Marvel Spotlight is an all-new way to experience some of the greatest heroes ever. But the best part is that we get to watch you interpret them in your own way as you expand the Marvel Universe into a whole new medium (yes, and *then* we can claim complete and utter world domination).

At Marvel we tell the stories of ordinary people doing extraordinary things and I can't wait to see what extraordinary things you'll bring to these stories. So now, if you'd indulge me, take a deep breath and say it with me, loud, so that they call down from hallowed halls of Asgard complaining about the noise: "Move over, Shakespeare! Take a seat, Chekhov! Here comes Marvel Spotlight!"

See ya in the funny books,

Joe Quesada
Chief Creative Officer
Marvel Entertainment, Inc.

## THE ORIGIN OF THOR & LOKI

Thor, God of Thunder, has spent most of his immortal life defending Earth and other realms from threats as Prince of Asgard, realm of the gods, and a founding member of The Avengers. He wields the mystical mallet Mjolnir with immense power and can summon the lightning and thunder... which comes in handy when he finds himself in trouble caused by his brother Loki, God of Mischief, whose tricks and schemes have often wreaked havoc across the realms!

## AUTHOR'S NOTE

When I was twelve, my life was forever changed during a slumber party in Rob Slifkin's basement. Someone handed me a copy of Marvel Comics' *G.I. Joe: A Real American Hero #21*, the silent issue. Within, our masked hero, Snake Eyes, infiltrates a castle guarded by the evil minions of COBRA to rescue his teammate Scarlet from the clutches of our masked villain, Storm Shadow. Panel after panel, the story unfolded with such economy and, dare I say it, kick-assery that I found myself holding my breath for twenty-two pages. In the end, as Storm Shadow watches Snake Eyes make his escape, we see that both hero and villain's sleeves have torn open, revealing on their forearms THE SAME CRYPTIC TATTOO!!!!! Mind. Blown. My tiny head swirled with questions. So began my weekly trips to the comics shop to find the answers. Weekly trips that introduced me to my first tribe: comic book geeks. Weekly trips that continue to this day.

When I was fifteen, my life was forever changed again when Shyaporn Theerakulstit convinced me to audition for the spring musical, *Oklahoma!* I was cast as one of the leads, Will Parker, opposite Amy Hartmann as Ado Annie. At rehearsals, I would draw comics in my big yellow sketch pad until one of my scenes was up, pop out my retainer, and then hop up on stage to sing and dance my little, fearless heart out. For all you romantics out there, my first kiss happened in a basement in the music department, rehearsing a scene in Act Two. The stage directions read, "Will and Annie kiss." Our musical director, Mr. Brill, just said, "Go ahead." I turned beet red, puckered up, and kissed Amy. Mind. Blown. So began my love affair with the stage. A love affair that introduced me to my second tribe: theater geeks. A love affair that continues to this day.

Writing *Hammered* was like stepping into a time machine, as if I were collaborating with my twelve- and fifteen-year-old selves. I experienced waves of giddiness akin to cracking open my first comic or kissing my first crush. Putting words in the mouths of these Marvel characters for budding comic book/theater geeks, to say, fearlessly, has been one of the greatest full-circle joys of my life.

So thank you Rob Slifkin, Shyaporn Theerakulstit, Amy Hartmann, and Mr. Brill. To me, you're the real American heroes.

Christian Borle

# CHARACTERS

## EARTH

**COMIC BOOK GEEK** – High school underclassman. May double as **LOKI**. Male identifying.

**JOCK** – High school upperclassman. May double as **THOR**. Male identifying.

**YEARBOOK EDITOR** – High school upperclassman, scholarly, focused on the future. May double as **SIF**. Female identifying.

## THE COSMIC VOID

**THOR ODINSON** – God of Thunder, nearing the end of his millennia-long life. May double as **ODIN**. Male identifying.

**ATLI** – Thor's youngest granddaughter, a hellcat. May double as **CUL**. Female identifying.

**ELLISIV** – Thor's middle granddaughter, a nurturer. May double as **HEIMDALL**. Female identifying.

**FRIGG** – Thor's eldest granddaughter, the pragmatist. May double as **HOENIR**. Female identifying.

## ASGARD

**THOR** – Teenage God of Thunder, son of Odin and Freyja. Male identifying.

**LOKI** – Teenage God of Mischief, Thor's younger adopted brother. Male identifying.

**FREYJA** – Queen of Asgard, Master of Courtly Etiquette, mother of Thor and Loki. Female identifying.

**ODIN** – King of Asgard, father of Thor and Loki. Male identifying.

**FANDRAL** – Thor's dashing cad of a pal. May double as **FORSETI**. Male identifying.

**VOLSTAGG** – Thor's friend, his appetite as big as his heart. Male identifying.

## INTERLUDE ONE
### The Cosmic Void

*(Silence. A field of stars illuminates the surface of a foreign moon. Sitting atop a throne of rock is* **THOR ODINSON,** *older than time, his beard white, his one good eye shut tight as he tosses fitfully, in the throes of a nightmare.)*

**THOR ODINSON.** My hammer... my hammer... in the name of all gods past and present... *(bolting awake)* WHITHER MY HAMMER???

> *(***THOR ODINSON** *reaches a desperate, splayed hand to the heavens, beckoning for his hammer, but is met with silence. He drops his hand, defeated, confused. Enter* **ATLI,** *his youngest granddaughter, a fiery spirit.)*

Ah, Jane, my dearest love. What have you done to your hair? I like it... not.

**ATLI.** How you flatter, Thor.

**THOR ODINSON.** *(suddenly suspicious)* Strange. How is it you haven't aged a day?

**ATLI.** Simple. I bench press thrice my own weight daily.

> *(Enter* **ELLISIV,** **ATLI***'s older sister, a calming presence.)*

**ELLISIV.** Enough mischief. Don't toy with him.

**ATLI.** Well, I do...

**THOR ODINSON.** *(looking between the two women, becoming agitated)* What devilry is this? Two Janes? Ah-HA! 'Tis the shape-shifting Skrulls returned to torment me! Prepare to taste the wrath of Thor, God of Thunder! Have at thee!

> *(***THOR ODINSON** *struggles to stand up but collapses, his age and body failing him.)*

**ELLISIV.** Hush, now...

*(Enter **FRIGG**, the eldest sister, regal and tough.)*

**THOR ODINSON.** A third hell-spawn!

**FRIGG.** Is he in another one of his states?

**ATLI.** We're at about an eight on the... *(whistles and does the "cuckoo" gesture)* ... meter.

**ELLISIV.** He was confusing us with his beloved bride, Jane Foster of Midgard.

**ATLI.** And calling out for his hammer. Again.

**THOR ODINSON.** Don't talk about me as if I'm not sitting right here. Who are you, then?

**FRIGG.** Do you not recognize us, your own granddaughters?

**THOR ODINSON.** *(haze in his eye seeming to lift, smiling)* My... granddaughters. Of course. Frigg, eldest and fiercest. Ellisiv, gentlest and wisest. And Atli, youngest and... I still don't like your hair.

**ATLI.** That's what I get? *(hiking a thumb at **ELLISIV**)* This one's basically wearing a bedsheet and I get fashion shade?

> *(**THOR ODINSON** bellows a hearty laugh, which turns into a cough.)*

**ELLISIV.** Calm yourself, Grandfather.

**THOR ODINSON.** *(taking in his surroundings)* What desolate throne is this?

**FRIGG.** A resting place of your own choosing at the torn edge of the universe.

**ELLISIV.** We come to bring you succor.

**ATLI.** Which is just a fancy way of saying "apple sauce." Are you hungry?

**THOR ODINSON.** To Hel with your sweet porridge! Thor Odinson does not gum his foods! *(suddenly hunting frantically for something around his throne)* Gods damn it, where is it?

**FRIGG.** Do you need your grabby-claw-reacher thing?

**ELLISIV.** The remote?

**THOR & LOKI.** *(through gritted teeth)* We brothers, we
princes Asgardian... loyal and royal and proud...
neither quarrel nor blunder can rend us asunder...
decree we thus far and loud.

> *(As the* **BOYS** *hold the hand shake,* **THOR**
> *smiles his perfect smile,* **LOKI** *fights back a
> grimace. Then...)*

**FREYJA.** He's doing the hand bone thing, isn't he?

**LOKI.** *(flashing his trademark smirk)* Why, Mother, that
would be tattling.

> *(The* **BOYS** *break and* **FREYJA** *wraps her arms
> around both of her sons maternally.)*

**FREYJA.** Enough. Both of you, off to your exams. Make me
proud.

> *(***LOKI** *starts to exit.)*

And Loki, a little less stealing, if you please.

**LOKI.** Borrowing, dear mother. Borrowing.

> *(***LOKI** *pulls the ball-peen hammer out of
> his tunic again.* **THOR** *checks his belt. No
> hammer. Before* **THOR** *can charge,* **LOKI** *drops
> the hammer and, flashing one last smile,
> bolts from the room.)*

**THOR.** That's right! Thou hadst better run!

> *(***FREYJA** *allows herself a laugh but then
> notices* **THOR**'s *brow furrowing as he picks up
> the hammer.)*

**FREYJA.** Thor, don't let these exams trouble you. Your
marks have shown great improvement these past few
years. No one expects you to...

**THOR.** Go on, Mother. Say it. No one expects me to what?

**FREYJA.** I mean to say, your destiny—

**THOR.** My destiny is to be nothing but a blunt instrument.
Useful. Strong. But dull.

**FREYJA.** You are not dull. Flame detailing on your gull-wing doors, hello! Serious, perhaps. But then, your father grew serious once he realized what weight would rest upon his shoulders. I remember one day he just... laughed less.

**THOR.** Is that why you favor Loki? He laughs more with each passing day.

**FREYJA.** Favor...? I see. I was foolish to think this was about your exams. You mark me now. I have two sons, two very different sons, who would both one day be King. I love you equally. But perhaps with different parts of my heart. *(pause)* Your brother looks up to you, you know.

**THOR.** Right.

**FREYJA.** He loves you.

**THOR.** He hates me.

**FREYJA.** You are wrong. You'll see. Be patient with him, Thor. Promise me.

**THOR.** I promise.

**FREYJA.** Good. Now. Hang up your rad tapestry and then go ace your exams.

**THOR.** "Rad"? Mom, no.

**FREYJA.** Lit?

**THOR.** That's not a thing anymore.

**FREYJA.** When you've lived five thousand years, you'll see. These things always come back around. 'Tis pretty sick.

**THOR.** Mom!

**FREYJA.** And so I take my leave.

> *(**FREYJA** exits with a regal curtsy. **THOR** laughs. Then, he digs back into his toolbox, finds a nail, and sticks it in his teeth. He picks up his tapestry and moves to the wall, assessing a spot to hang it, hammer in hand. He looks at the ball-peen hammer... then slowly, triumphantly, daydreaming of Mjolnir, raises it in the air. Blackout.)*

knows it's true. That might explain his propensity for... mischief. But remember, my son, there is room for a bit of mischief in life. The time will come for seriousness... when you are crowned king. *(off* THOR*'s stunned reaction)* This look you make! Would you begrudge an old man for stating what is so obvious?

THOR. No, Father. It's just—

ODIN. Your destiny. Now, look, you've made me serious. How do you feel about your exams today?

THOR. Nervous.

ODIN. It is to be expected. Have you studied well?

THOR. Until the runes turned blurry on the page.

ODIN. Then your work here is done. A bit of fatherly advice, then. And by my right hand if you tell your mother I said so, I'll deny it. *(checking to make sure the coast is clear, producing a mead skin from his robes)* A cask or two of mead drunk before any important test quenches the belly, lubricates the mind, and reminds you that, even in the darkest of times, life is meant to be celebrated. Trust me, boy. When I vanquished the Frost Giants and made parley with King Laufey to bring about a lasting truce, I was half in the bag on Jotunheimrish ambrosia. I say, if you're old enough to fight like a king, you're old enough to drink like a king. *(clocking* THOR*'s hesitation)* Look me in my one good eye and tell me true, have you never snuck a gulp or two to give you the courage to ask that comely mammoth trainer in the stables to dance?

THOR. *(a bashful grin)* Greta.

ODIN. Ho HO! We are more alike with every passing day. *(dangling the skin in front of* THOR*, a mischievous smile dancing on his face)* Lighten up, my boy! 'Tis an order from your King.

> *(A twinkle grows in* THOR*'s eyes. Blackout.)*

## EPISODE THREE
### The Lecture Hall

*(Lights up on a raised dais. Five stoic*
**MASTERS** *preside:* **HEIMDALL, HOENIR, FORSETI,**
**CUL,** *and* **QUEEN FREYJA,** *sitting center.* **THE**
**HERALD** *stands attending to one side.* **LOKI**
*stands before the dais, finishing his exams.)*

**LOKI.** 'Tis a trick question, My Queen. If a visiting
dignitary has a therapy cow on his lap at the Feast of
Skadi, then no salad forks are used. Etiquette dictates
that guests should eat with their hands.

*(The* **MASTERS** *murmur their assent.)*

**FREYJA.** Very good, Loki. Lay by a moment while we
confer.

**THE HERALD.** The Masters will now confer! *(blat)* I'm back!

*(***LOKI** *shifts nervously as the* **MASTERS** *put*
*their heads together, whispering. Satisfied,*
**FREYJA** *nods at* **THE HERALD.***)*

The Masters will now pronounce your results!
Heimdall, Master of History! *(blat)*

**HEIMDALL.** Outstanding.

**THE HERALD.** Hoenir, Master of Runeology! *(blat)*

**HOENIR.** Outstanding.

**THE HERALD.** Queen Freyja, Master of Courtly Etiquette!
*(blat)*

**FREYJA.** Outstanding.

**THE HERALD.** Forseti, Master of Mathematics! *(blat)*

**FORSETI.** Outstanding.

**THE HERALD.** Cul, Master of Combat!

*(***THE HERALD***'s next blat is preempted as* **CUL**
*snatches the trumpet and bends it over one*
*knee.)*

I'm only trying to do my job.

**CUL.** Do it... quieter.

**THE HERALD.** *(in a stage whisper)* Cul, Master of Combat!

**CUL.** Poor. If war breaks out, I encourage you to hide in the cellars. Just embarrassing. My infant child could best you in fisticuffs and he still suckles at—

**FREYJA.** Thank you, Master Cul! We all have our strengths and weaknesses. I strain to remember seeing you pick up a book. All in all, well done, Loki. You graduate to form five with flying colors.

**LOKI.** *(bowing low)* Thank you, Masters.

**THE HERALD.** *(still a stage whisper)* Presenting the next examinee... Thor!

> *(As **LOKI** exits, **THOR** bounds in, loose and smiling. He stops his brother with a clumsy paw, his volume a little high given their close proximity.)*

**THOR.** Brother! Hey! How did it go?

**LOKI.** Fairly well.

**THOR.** *(wrapping **LOKI** in a bear hug)* You're so smart. Hey, I'm sorry about this morning. You know me, I get a little... *(pantomimes growling, false bravado)* Are we good?

**LOKI.** *(conscious of the somewhat bewildered **ONLOOKERS**)* I am good. Are you good? You seem... sweaty.

**THOR.** Never better!

**FREYJA.** Ahem. While it warms the heart to see such a display of fraternal affection, perhaps we could commence with the examination?

**THOR.** Of course! *(ushering **LOKI** out with a hard clap on the back)* Hey, I'll see you later.

**LOKI.** *(exiting)* Not if I see you first.

**THOR.** *(turning his attention to the **MASTERS**, chuckling)* That guy, am I right? *(bowing low, almost stumbling, but recovering with a jaunty skip)* Masters. Mommy.

**HEIMDALL.** I see you are in a merry mood today, young Thor. Shall we begin? Question one—

**THOR.** When do we get to the fighting?!

**FREYJA.** Thor, such impudence is unbecoming.

**THOR.** I meant no offense, Masters. Only, a wise woman once told me I was growing too serious. So let's have a little fun!

**CUL.** Hold!

> (**CUL** *steps down from the dais and approaches* **THOR**. *They stand face to face.*)

**THOR.** Hi.

**CUL.** *(inhaling deeply)* Mint leaf. *(sniffing again)* And something else.

**THOR.** Wheat grass. I've been on a bit of a juice kick of late. Clears the mind. And the colon, know what'm say'n?

**CUL.** I say we grant young Thor's wish and... how did you put it... have a little fun. Let's skip to the combat trial.

> (**THE HERALD** *lifts trumpet excitedly, remembers, lowers it.*)

**THE HERALD.** *(stage whisper)* Let the combat trial commence!

> (**CUL** *grabs two wooden practice swords and tosses one to* **THOR**, *who takes a couple of swings, showing off.*)

**THOR.** Who shall be the sacrificial lamb brought to slaughter?

**CUL.** You will face the only student yet to be bested in today's trials.

> (**CUL** *nods to* **THE HERALD**.)

**THE HERALD.** *(still a stage whisper)* Presenting... Lady Sif.

> (*As* **SIF** *enters,* **CUL** *tosses her the other sword, which she catches in stride, without looking. She takes a couple of swings, limbering up.* **THOR** *and* **SIF** *circle each other, speaking sotto voce.*)

**THOR.** I promise I'll go easy on you.

**SIF**. From the smell of you, friend, that would be your second mistake of the day.

**CUL**. The rules are simple. No shots to the head. Beyond that, fight until one of you is on the ground. Begin!

> (**THOR** and **SIF** *fight. The staccato clacking of the swords is interrupted occasionally by their verbal sparring. They are evenly matched.*)

**SIF**. Your footing is sloppy.

**THOR**. I'm trying something new. It's called "The Norse Pony."

> (**THOR** *distracts her with a dance move. Then,* **THOR** *steals a page from his brother's playbook by mockingly repeating what* **SIF** *says almost at the same time.*)

**SIF & THOR**. Stop acting the fool and fight.

> (**THOR** *backs* **SIF** *up with a series of out-of-control swings.*)

You're embarrassing yourself.

**CUL**. Enough chatter! Finish it.

**THOR**. As you wish!

> (**THOR** *spins and with a mighty swing cracks* **SIF** *across the jaw. The* **MASTERS** *stand, letting out a shocked gasp.* **SIF** *swoons but does not go down.* **THOR***, stunned, approaches her.*)

Sif, I... I'm sorry. I didn't mean—

> (**SIF** *lets* **THOR** *get close. Then, with whirlwind dexterity and precision, puts him on the ground. She stands over him, her sword in his face.* **CUL** *steps forward, clapping.*)

**CUL**. You were right about one thing, Thor. That was fun.

> (**FREYJA** *descends from the dais.*)

**FREYJA**. This is no joke. Sif, are you injured?

**SIF.** A gentle crack across the jaw was well worth the victory, My Queen. I would worry more about your son's bruised ego.

**THOR.** *(getting to his feet, humiliated)* 'Twas pure luck. She never would have bested me if—

**CUL.** If you weren't drunk? I can smell the mead seeping from his pores.

**FREYJA.** Hold your tongue, Cul. How dare you level such an accusation at my—

**THOR.** He speaks the truth, Mother.

*(A pall falls over the **MASTERS**.)*

**FREYJA.** I have no words to express my utter disappointment. And yet, how unlike you this is. Did someone put you up to this? Did Fandral pour honey into your ear? Herald, call the students back. We will get to the bottom of this.

*(**THE HERALD** bows and makes for the exit...)*

**THOR.** It was Father.

**FREYJA.** Oh, Thor...

**THOR.** Truly! Leave Fandral and the rest out of this. It was the King's wish to see me—

**FREYJA.** Stop. Set aside for a moment the preposterous notion that your father would encourage such wanton foolishness...

**THOR.** But he did! He gave me—

**FREYJA.** Enough! Heimdall, Seer of All, tell me. Where is Odin now?

**HEIMDALL.** *(looking into the middle distance)* My Queen, Odin yet sleeps in his meditative trance. As he has without interruption for the last fortnight. The royal guards have orders to stand outside his chambers so that none would disturb him until the ides of spring.

**THOR.** But that's impossible!

**FREYJA.** Would you cast doubt upon Heimdall's all-seeing eye? *(off **THOR**'s silence)* And so. Do you wish to amend

your story? This ill-begotten attempt to shield your
friends, while commendable, is—

**THOR**. It was my idea and mine alone. I am a fool. Forgive
me.

**FREYJA**. You have much to learn, Thor. Let this be the
lesson for today. A drunk prince is an embarrassment.
A lying prince is not worthy to succeed. And so, you
fail.

*(Blackout.)*

## EPISODE FOUR
### Thor's Bedroom

> (**THOR** *paces back and forth in front of the now-hanging tapestry of the Asgard 3000z like a caged, confused animal. He lets out a wall-shaking wail of frustration.* **LOKI** *pops his head out from behind the left side of the tapestry.*)

**LOKI**. Hey. How'd it go?

**THOR**. You play with fire, Loki. I am in no mood for your smug barbs.

> (**LOKI** *pops his head back.*)

Leave me alone, I warn you.

> (*As* **THOR** *storms away he hears a familiar voice from behind the tapestry.*)

**ODIN**. *(offstage)* Poor, pathetic Thor.

> (**THOR** *whirls to see* **ODIN** *step out from behind the right side of the tapestry.*)

Hello, brother mine. Is that hangover settling in yet? I never touch the stuff myself. You should see your face! There's smoke coming out of your ears as you try to puzzle, so hard, how am I doing this? Has a shape-shifting Skrull replaced your cherished brother? It's simpler than that. While you've been daydreaming of chariots and sucking up to Mother and flirting with mammoth trainers, I've been taking some lessons of my own. Lesson one: a weak mind... thaaat's you... is easily manipulated by a cunning one... thaaat's me. Basic trickery, really. Just a bit of mischief. Not as blunt as a hammer but just as effective at yielding results, no?

> (**ODIN** *ducks back behind the tapestry as* **LOKI** *appears again on the other side.*)

**LOKI**. Mark me now, Thor. One day you may well be worthy of wielding a magic hammer, true. But my brain is my hammer. And I am already worthy enough to wield it. Toodles!

>   (**LOKI** *exits behind the tapestry with a jaunty wave. In a rage,* **THOR** *strides to the tapestry and yanks it down.* **LOKI** *has disappeared. Blackout.*)

## INTERLUDE TWO
### The Cosmic Void

*(Lights up on* **THOR ODINSON**, *energized,
sitting forward in his throne. His*
**GRANDDAUGHTERS** *kneel before him, rapt.)*

**ATLI.** You know, on Midgard they have a name for a story
like that.

**THOR ODINSON.** A myth?

**ATLI.** An Afterschool Special.

**THOR ODINSON.** 'Tis the truth!

**ELLISIV.** Grandfather, a question. Why did you believe so
easily that Odin would steer you down such a reckless
path?

**THOR ODINSON.** Odin was always King first, father
second. When I saw the smile dancing on his face as
he handed me that mead skin, it was as if we were...
peers for a moment. What son doesn't yearn for such
a stolen moment? Loki understood that. And used
it against me. Gods, I hated him that day. *(getting
a twinkle in his eye)* But revenge, two years in the
making and war hammer now firmly in hand, can be
sweet.

**ELLISIV.** Tell us, Grandfather.

**ATLI.** Another story? I was hoping for a snack, maybe a
quick pee.

**THOR ODINSON.** Hold your tongue and your bladder,
firebrand, and humor an old man.

**ATLI.** Fiiiiine-uh. But maybe a little more blood and guts
this time?

**THOR ODINSON.** How like Loki you are in your appetite
for destruction. *(looking at her with... suspicion?)*
Curious.

**FRIGG.** 'Twas sweet revenge that jogged your memory,
Grandfather. Lay on.

**THOR ODINSON.** It all started... with a firecracker.

> *(As* **THOR** *snaps his fingers, a loud crack.
> Blackout.)*

## EPISODE FIVE
### The Mine, Two Years Later

*(Cacophony! An avalanche or a rockslide
or both. As the sound subsides with a
denouement of pebbles settling... lights up.*
**THOR** *and* **LOKI** *are trapped, mashed against
each other, in a claustrophobic rock crevice,
covered in dirt and dust. For a moment,
it's hard to tell whether or not they've been
crushed to death. Then...)*

**THOR.** What... was that?

**LOKI.** Cave-in.

**THOR.** Yes, but what triggered it?

**LOKI.** Gods only know.

**THOR.** Can you move?

**LOKI.** Not an inch. You?

> *(**THOR** strains mightily. Nothing.)*

**THOR.** I'm wedged. I can't get any leverage. Damn!

**LOKI.** Save your breath.

**THOR.** Of course. Thank you, Brother.

**LOKI.** No, you're blowing it right on me. Don't you brush?

> *(**THOR** blows hot breath in **LOKI**'s face.)*

You're a child.

> *(An ominous rumble above them.)*

**THOR.** Surely someone heard. They're probably already
digging.

**LOKI.** Did you tell anyone where we were going?

**THOR.** No. You?

**LOKI.** I'm not much of a gabber.

> *(**THOR** chuckles.)*

What?

**THOR.** Loki... you monologue.

**LOKI**. I do not.

**THOR**. Runt, please. You narrated your first steps.

**LOKI**. How many times do I have to say it, I'm LITHE!

(*Another rumble overhead.*)

**THOR**. Fine, have it your way, Your Litheness. (*then*) Well? What now?

**LOKI**. Um, this seems like the perfect time to call your precious hammer. How do you do it, just whistle a magic little tune or something?

**THOR**. Don't you think I already thought of that? I've been clenching this whole time.

**LOKI**. Ah, it's more of a clenching thing. Got it.

**THOR**. We must be buried too deep for it to feel my summons. Any other bright ideas?

**LOKI**. HELP!!!!! HEEEEEEEEEEEEELP!!!!!!!!

**THOR**. That's it?

**LOKI**. Got a better idea?

**THOR**. WE'RE DOWN HERE!!!!!!!!

**THOR & LOKI**. HEEEEEEEEEEEEEEEEELP!!!!!!!!!!!!

(**THOR** *and* **LOKI** *hold for a response. Silence.*)

**THOR**. This is ridiculous. We're gods.

**LOKI**. That doesn't make us invulnerable. Mayhaps you've heard of a little place called Valhalla where gods go when they die?

**THOR**. Wow. This got dark fast.

**LOKI**. You know me. Gallows humor is my bailiwick.

(*A beat.*)

You don't know what "bailiwick" means, do you?

**THOR**. Of course I know what "bailiwick" means.

**LOKI**. Go on. Tell me what it means.

**THOR**. It means... (*blows another hot breath in* **LOKI**'s *face*)

**LOKI**. That's what I thought.

(*A beat. A gentle rumble.*)

**THOR**. Fine. Educate me. If that will make you feel better.

**LOKI**. Put it this way... strutting around like a pompous ass is your bailiwick. Finding new and puerile ways to demean me is your bailiwick. Pretending like I'm not your brother is your bailiwick.

**THOR**. Ah.

**LOKI**. You don't know what "puerile" means either, do you? *(silence)* I'm joking! For someone with all that muscle you have awfully thin skin.

**THOR**. Everything with you is a joke.

**LOKI**. This isn't a joke though, is it? We're trapped.

**THOR**. I think so, yes.

> *(Driving the point home, another rumble overhead.)*

**LOKI**. It's my fault.

**THOR**. What?

**LOKI**. This. I lured you into this mine with the promise of finding the perfect gift for your lady love.

**THOR**. She's not my "lady love." We're just... dating.

**LOKI**. That's the part you're hung up on? I'm telling you this is my fault! I set a booby trap. We trudge down here in the filth, you by chance find the perfect sapphire with which to woo Greta and as you reach out for it... BANG! I only meant to shock you.

**THOR**. You said "booby."

**LOKI**. Puerile, I rest my case. *(then)* Thor, hear me. I'm sorry. I never expected... this.

**THOR**. I know you're sorry. And I know it was all a trap! I mean, you're you! You really think I'm an idiot, don't you?

**LOKI**. Yes, you're an idiot...

**THOR**. That's what I thought.

**LOKI**. No, you're an idiot because... I would give anything to be you.

**THOR**. Even now with the jests?

**LOKI**. No. No more jests. No more games. If this is the end, let's at least talk to each other brother to brother.

*(Another rumble.)*

**THOR**. Okay, I'll start. I'm scared. We're running out of air. I can feel it.

**LOKI**. Me too.

**THOR**. And I'm sorry, too. I've been a bully to you.

**LOKI**. You're just—

**THOR**. Let me finish. I know I have my strengths. I also know I have everything served up for me on a silver platter. Mother and Father, as much as they try, are not... fair when it comes to you and me. I don't know why. But I confess... deep down... I relish it.

**LOKI**. I would too.

**THOR**. I hate how smart you are.

**LOKI**. I hate how strong you are.

**THOR**. I hate how funny you are.

**LOKI**. I hate how noble you are.

**THOR**. I hate your stupid cool hair.

**LOKI**. I hate your stupid handsome face.

**THOR**. What are you talking about? You're handsome!

**LOKI**. Brother, nobody wants to be handsome in an "off-beat" way.

*(**THOR** and **LOKI** laugh together.)*

**THOR**. We should conserve our breath.

*(A beat. More rumbling above.)*

**LOKI**. How are things going with you and Greta?

**THOR**. We've yet to even kiss.

**LOKI**. What's the hold up?

**THOR**. I just don't... feel like myself around her. I'm always putting something on.

**LOKI**. Which begs the age-old question, what is the deal you and Sif?

**THOR**. Odin's beard! Why can't everyone let that go? She's my friend. Can't a man and a woman just be friends?

**LOKI**. Don't ask me. I don't have a lot of experience with friends, period.

    *(A beat.)*

**THOR**. Hey, what about you? Isn't there... anyone you... you know...

**LOKI**. Who would have me?

**THOR**. You're an idiot. *(then)* You're so cool. So "mysterious." Some brotherly advice? I think you just need to—

**LOKI**. Don't say—

**THOR & LOKI**. Put yourself/myself out there.

**LOKI**. Easy for you to say. You can call down thunder.

**THOR**. And you make magic with mischief. That business with you convincing me you were Father two years ago was brilliant.

**LOKI**. Thor. You can call down thunder.

**THOR**. I heard you.

**LOKI**. No. Now. Call down thunder and lightning and shatter this wall of rock. Time is running short. Do it.

**THOR**. Brother. It might—

**LOKI**. Kill me? Mayhaps. Death seems slightly inevitable for both of us at this point. But you'd live. You're strong enough.

**THOR**. Loki...

**LOKI**. I want you to. Save yourself. If you're so smart, tell me. Why should both of us die?

    *(Silence.)*

**THOR**. No. I could never live with myself. If this is the end then we will meet it together. As brothers. *(struggling to free his right hand, offering it to* **LOKI***)* Say it with me.

**LOKI**. What?

**THOR**. You know.

**LOKI**. By gods, you're sentimental. That's how you want to go out?

**THOR.** For absolute sooth, dude.

> (**LOKI** *frees his right hand and clasps* **THOR***'s.*)

**THOR & LOKI.** We brothers, we princes Asgardian... loyal and royal and proud...

**THOR.** Neither quarrel nor blunder—

**LOKI.** No, neither mischief nor thunder!

**THOR.** Good tweak!

**THOR & LOKI.** Neither mischief nor thunder can rend us asunder... decree we thus far and loud.

> (*A beat.*)

**LOKI.** Thank you for not crushing my hand bones.

**THOR.** Least I could do.

> (*The rumble overhead grows even louder. The walls seem to shake now.*)

**LOKI.** This could be it. I feel surprisingly calm. *(then)* I love you, Brother.

**THOR.** Aaaaaaaaaaand... there it is.

**LOKI.** There what is?

**THOR.** I knew there was more to you than mischief!

**LOKI.** Well, looks like that'll be our little secret!

**THOR.** Or...

> (**THOR** *whistles a magic little tune.*)

**LOKI.** What are you...?

**THOR.** Wait for it...

> (*Crash! Mjolnir bursts through the ceiling of rock and lands in* **THOR***'s hand. A pool of light from above bathes him and the hammer in heroic light.* **THOR** *and* **LOKI** *look at each other and burst out into joyous laughter.*)

**LOKI.** You could do that the whole time???

**THOR.** *(with a satisfied smile)* Gotcha.

**LOKI.** I hate you.

**THOR.** You looooooooove me.

**LOKI.** I've got to hand it to you... well played.

**THOR.** Thank you. Pretty proud of myself. Hey, good talk.

**LOKI.** Yep. Overdue. So you really do just whistle a magic little tune? Isn't that a little effete?

**THOR.** No, that was just for show. It really is more of a clenching thing.

**LOKI.** Good to know. Well, what are you waiting for, brother mine? Get hammering!

> (**THOR** *smiles with his perfect teeth and looks at Mjolnir. Then slowly, triumphantly raises it in the air. Then...*)

You don't know what "effete" means, do you?

> (*Blackout.*)

## INTERLUDE THREE
### The Cosmic Void

**THOR ODINSON.** *(smiles serenely in reverie)* Good talk. *(noticing* **GRANDDAUGHTERS***)* I never got to say goodbye to him, to say thank you. Loki saved us all in the end, didn't he?

**FRIGG.** *(getting a little emotional)* Aye, Grandfather. He gave of himself so that we all may live. A little longer.

**ELLISIV.** *(giving into the emotion too)* One thing is certain. He is in Valhalla now.

**ATLI.** *(joining in the emotion)* Because of his noble sacrifice, his name is spoken now alongside the pantheon of the mightiest heroes.

**THOR ODINSON.** He always saw the long game, that... runt.

> *(The* **GRANDDAUGHTERS** *suddenly drop any pretense of emotion.)*

**FRIGG.** Runt?

**ELLISIV.** "Lithe" is the more fitting description.

**ATLI.** Lithe bordering on sexy, by all accounts.

> *(***THOR ODINSON** *suddenly stands on his own two feet for the first time, strong, his old heroic self.)*

**THOR ODINSON.** All right, enough, brother mine! Thou art pushing it now. "Sexy"? We agreed you were handsome in an off-beat way. That's as far as I'm willing to go!

**FRIGG.** "Brother mine"? Grandfather...

**ELLISIV.** His vapors have returned stronger than ever...

**ATLI.** I'm standing by "sexy."

**THOR ODINSON.** *(smiling)* Imitating father is one thing. Tell me, Loki, what mischief did you learn in Valhalla to split yourself into three maidens?

> *(The* **GRANDDAUGHTERS** *fade gracefully away and, in a bit of stage magic, teenage* **LOKI** *takes their place.)*

**LOKI.** What gave me away?

**THOR ODINSON.** A dozen subtle things only a brother would notice. But you never could stand silent while someone called you a runt.

**LOKI.** Too true. Too true.

**THOR ODINSON.** But why not just appear to me as yourself? Why choose the guise of my granddaughters?

**LOKI.** *(beat)* WHY DO I DO ANYTHING???

> (**LOKI** *and* **THOR ODINSON** *suddenly laugh together, long and hard. The laughter abates.*)

**THOR ODINSON.** *(sits again, wiping a tear from his one good eye)* It feels good to laugh. *(then)* Loki?

**LOKI.** Yes?

**THOR ODINSON.** You are kind to visit me here. I'm sorry I couldn't save you. I tried.

**LOKI.** Idiot. You did save me. Long ago. Forgive yourself, Thor. Rest with me now in Valhalla. Come on, I'm bored. And the Jotunheimrish ambrosia flows from cascading fountains. You're certainly old enough for it now.

**THOR ODINSON.** Is Jane there?

**LOKI.** She is... elsewhere. At peace.

**THOR ODINSON.** I will never be at peace until I join her. I am my true self with her.

**LOKI.** I know. But your eternal destinies lie along different paths, Brother. I'm sorry.

> *(A beat.)*

**THOR ODINSON.** Loki, I want to tell you...

**LOKI.** I can always tell when you're about to get sentimental.

> (**LOKI** *does the thing where he irritates* **THOR ODINSON** *by mockingly repeating whatever he says almost at the same time.*)

**THOR ODINSON & LOKI.**
>You would have been a worthy king, in the end.
>Stop that.
>Seriously, I hate when you do this.

**THOR ODINSON.** Will I see you back here tomorrow?

**LOKI.** Valhalla's pretty happening, but I should have a free
>window between bottomless brunch and unicorn polo,
>sure.

**THOR ODINSON.** Will I know it's you, Brother?

**LOKI.** Sometimes you figure out the game pretty fast.

**THOR ODINSON.** And the other times?

**LOKI.** I just sit here quietly and watch you gum apple
>sauce.

>>(**THOR ODINSON,** *on the verge of nodding off*
>>*now, manages a smirk.*)

**THOR ODINSON.** I would sleep now.

>>(*As* **THOR ODINSON***'s eye closes for the shortest*
>>*second,* **LOKI** *disappears.*)

>Loki, if I never said it enough…

>>(**THOR ODINSON** *forces his eye open, only to*
>>*realize he is alone. He sinks back into his*
>>*stone throne with a small smile. As the lights*
>>*fade on* **THOR ODINSON,** *the lights come up*
>>*on the* **JOCK** *sitting on the lip of the stage*
>>*reading his* Thor *comic. For one magical*
>>*moment we are in both worlds.*)

## EPILOGUE
### Earth

**THOR ODINSON & JOCK**. "That's right... thou hadst better run."

> *(At the very moment the lights fade out on* **THOR ODINSON**, *a bespectacled* **YEARBOOK EDITOR** *rushes by, in time to overhear the* **JOCK**.*)*

**YEARBOOK EDITOR**. Excuse me, I was not running. I was walking with extreme intention.

**JOCK**. No, I was just... reading aloud. To myself. Like ya do.

**YEARBOOK EDITOR**. What, pray tell, are you reading? Aloud.

**JOCK**. You sound surprised that I can read at all.

**YEARBOOK EDITOR**. Issues much? Just a question. What are you reading?

**JOCK**. *(a skeptical beat, then)* A comic. They're not all about sword-fighting, you know. I mean, there's some sword-fighting. But this one's actually about love.

**YEARBOOK EDITOR**. Oh, brother.

**JOCK**. And friendship. I'm embarrassed, I don't know your name.

**YEARBOOK EDITOR**. It's Jane. I know yours... Donald.

**JOCK**. It is written on my clothing. Like a pre-schooler.

**YEARBOOK EDITOR**. *(shyly)* Go, Thunderbolts!

> *(The* **JOCK** *offers up the comic.)*

**JOCK**. Well, I'm passing this on. Jane. I've already read it twice. Because, and I say this proudly, I... am a geek.

> *(The moment the* **YEARBOOK EDITOR** *grasps it, they mirror – not too literally – the tableau of Michelangelo's fresco* The Creation of Adam. *On the blackout, an electric guitar shreds a heart-jolting rock 'n' roll riff which culminates with a crack of thunder.)*

### End of Play

# GLOSSARY

Below are definitions and pronunciations of Norse names and other less common words found on the page numbers in parentheses.

**Aegirian** (11): Named after Aegir, the Norse God of the Sea. Pronounced ee-JEER-ee-un.

**Alfheim** (47): One of the Nine Realms in Norse mythology. Pronounced ALF-heim.

**Asgard** (IV, 1, 2, 5, 7, 8, 9, 22, 30, 38, 40, 41, 44, 45, 46, 47, 48): Realm of the gods. Pronounced AZ-gard.

**Bailiwick** (26): One's sphere of experience or expertise. Pronounced BAY-luh-wick.

**Bestla** (47): Mother of Odin. Name means "wife." Pronounced BEST-lah.

**Bragi** (11): Norse God of Poetry and Music. Pronounced BRAH-gee.

**Effete** (31): Affected, overrefined, and ineffectual.

**Frost Giants** (15): Inhabitants of Jotunheim, enemies of Asgard.

**Hel** (4): Helheim. One of the Nine Realms. Norse underworld, where many of the dead dwell.

**Jotunheim** (15, 33, 47): One of the Nine Realms. Home of the Frost Giants. Pronounced YO-ten-heim.

**Laufey** (15): King of the Frost Giants, enemy of Odin. Pronounced LAW-fay.

**Midgard** (4, 12, 24, 46, 48): Earth, one of the Nine Realms.

**Mjolnir** (V, 2, 5, 8, 10, 30, 31, 38, 48): Thor's magic war hammer, one of the most fearsome and powerful weapons in existence. Pronounced MYOHL-neer.

**Muspelheim** (47): One of the Nine Realms. Pronounced MOOSE-pehl-heim.

**Nifelheim** (47): One of the Nine Realms. Pronounced NEE-fuhl-heim.

**Perrikus** (5): One of the Dark Gods who invaded Asgard. Pronounced PAIR-i-kus.

**Pietà** (38): An image of the Virgin Mary holding the dead body of her son, Jesus Christ, on her lap or in her arms.

**Puerile** (27, 41): Childishly silly and trivial. Pronounced PURE-ile.

**Ragnarok** (5): The cataclysmic destruction of the cosmos and everything in it. Pronounced RAG-na-rock.

**Runeology** (IX, 13, 16): Pronounced roon-AW-luh-gee.

**Skadi** (16): Norse giantess and Goddess of Bow-Hunting, Winter, and Mountains. Pronounced SKAH-dee.

**Skrulls** (3, 22): Polymorphic enemies of Asgard.

**Succor** (4): Support and assistance in times of hardship or distress. Pronounced SUH-ker.

**Svartalfheim** (47): One of the Nine Realms. Pronounced ZVAHR-talf-heim.

**Tyr** (12): Commander of the Einherjar, the Asgardian army. Pronounced TEER.

**Valhalla** (26, 32, 33, 34): The palatial hall of honorable slain warriors who live blissfully under the leadership of Odin. Pronounced val-HALL-uh.

**Vanaheim** (47): One of the Nine Realms. Pronounced VAH-nah-HEIM.

**Yggdrasil** (46): The World Tree that connects all the Nine Realms. Pronounced IG-druh-suhl.

# PRODUCTION NOTES
By Christian Borle

The following pages offer staging, design, and
performance suggestions to inform your production
of *Hammered*. For more tips and guidance on how to
approach the Marvel Spotlight plays in production, visit
MarvelSpotlightPlays.com.

The staging of *Hammered* can be as literal as budget and
space will allow or as suggestive and abstract as needed.
One of the most useful tools will be sound effects.

### On *The Creation of Adam*

The image of Michelangelo's fresco *The Creation of Adam*
in the Prologue and Epilogue need not be, as is suggested
in the stage directions, literal. It's a moment. No need to
make a meal out of it. It's simply the outstretched passing
of the comic book baton. Ideally, the blackout and the
guitar riff should be cued the second contact is made.

### On Stage Combat

The stage combat between Thor and Sif should be catnip
for high school students but it need not be elaborate or
dangerous. For tips on how to stage choreographed fights
efficiently and safely, refer to MarvelSpotlightPlays.com.

### On the Tapestry

The hanging tapestry of the Asgard 3000z should be
large enough to hide two actors to accomplish the ol'
switcheroo of Loki becoming Odin. Please encourage
budding set designers or art students to go nuts on
the design. It should be the Asgardian equivalent of a
Lamborghini poster.

### On the Cave-In

The cave-in can be either a literal, cramped set which
somehow cracks open to reveal Mjolnir, or simply two
actors entangled *Pietà*-style in a pool of light. I think

there's something beautiful in the situation forcing these brothers/actors into a physically intimate position, which ultimately leads to the emotional intimacy in the scene. It can and should be appropriately awkward and poetic at the same time. (If the stage picture elicits giggles from the younger members of the audience, even better, I say. There's a lesson to be learned here.)

## On Loki's Final Trick

The "bit of stage magic" suggested as the granddaughters fade away and Loki reveals himself at the end can be accomplished by some creative thinking, a thunder and lightning strobe effect, perhaps, or just a clean bit of choreography as the three sisters make their dignified exit in unison and Loki takes their place. It needn't dazzle.

## On the Throne (heh)

Thor Odinson's throne presents a challenge that I hope will lead to some creative problem-solving. The interlude scenes in The Cosmic Void should be considered "in one," a classic term of theater craft. Historically, an "in one" scene took place downstage of the curtain as the scenery was being changed behind the curtain smoothing out and speeding up transitions. That's the goal here.

Whether the throne is placed off to the side or set high above the action (if you have access to, say, scaffolding), it should be an anchor we return to with a simple lighting cue. The less time it takes to go from The Interludes to The Episodes, the better.

Additionally, it's more effective for Thor Odinson to stay planted in his throne rather than roam around. It is a position of absolute power, even though his powers are clearly fading. Keeping him seated makes the moments when he tries to stand up (and then ultimately does) more impactful. Remember, he's, like, 5,000 years old.

### On The Herald's Trumpet

Use a plastic vuvuzela. They're cheap online. Wrap it in tin foil. It's even cheaper. Have fun with how Cul might "bend" or "break" it when the Herald's blats become too much.

### On Pacing

The first note is... take out the pauses. The second note is... protect the pauses. In general, the play should move. While there is a lot of ornate language and dense exposition to wade through, give the audience the benefit of the doubt that they are listening. Shakespeare said, "Speak the speech, I pray you... trippingly on the tongue." Good advice.

To that end, throughout the writing process, I took great care deciding when and how to use pauses, beats, silences, ellipses, and italics. They are all intentional, as are the stage directions and the parentheticals before character dialogue. Why are they all there? What do they all mean? The answers to those two questions are the road map to the rhythm of the play.

### On Comedy

I have endeavored to make *Hammered* a comedy. I certainly want the audience to have a few chuckles. The problem with comedy is, what you or I find funny, they might not find funny. There is no magical formula. So good luck! Here's my one tip to the actors: Protect the line after the laugh (should there be any).

### On Language

Language is, for me, the heart and soul of the play. The interplay between the formality of Asgardian wordplay and contemporary parlance is half if not all the fun.

It is my hope that students will relish learning new words within the context of this hip Marvel world. Googling Shakespeare references can feel like homework. This should have the "spoonful of sugar" effect of reading a comic book. It's all "CRACKS" and "POWS" until someone drops the word "puerile."

Actors should be encouraged to chew the language up. These are *gods* talking, after all. Hopefully the story is imbued with enough recognizable humanity, but the world of Asgard should feel like a heightened place. Much of the humor derives from coming off a grandiloquent, rococo run of words and landing on an anachronistic "dude" or a contemporary "am I right?" These shifts should be leaned into, highlighted, and lifted. Check out the Glossary (p. 36-37) for some quick Asgardian definitions and pronunciations to get you started.

# BEYOND THE STAGE

Facilitating a productive rehearsal process isn't just about having clear rehearsal plans, it's also about meaningful engagement and ensuring the well-being of your cast. It's important your cast feels physically, emotionally, and artistically safe throughout the rehearsal process. The following pages include resources to help:

- In-Rehearsal Discussion Starters
- Rehearsal Exercises
- Post-Show Talkbacks

For best practices on stage combat and to ensure the physical safety of your performers, ideas on how to make the Marvel Universe theatrical, and additional exercises to connect to the world of comics, go to MarvelSpotlightPlays.com.

### In-Rehearsal Discussion Starters

Throughout the rehearsal process, help your cast make deeper connections to the play and their characters using the following prompts:

- The characters approach the stress of exams in different ways, with varied success. What constructive ways have you found for handling stress?
- Thor juggles expectations from parents, school, and friends. How does he lose, and find, the balance? How do you?
- What about Thor and Loki's sibling rivalry do you relate to? What are the benefits and drawbacks of rivalry?

The director's job is not only to helm the artistic vision of the show, but also to assist actors in developing a bond as an ensemble, introduce them to the world of the play, and guide them to join the storytelling process. Below are a variety of exercises that will help with that. For even more rehearsal exercises, visit MarvelSpotlightPlays.com.

## MY HAMMER!

*Use this to:* *help ensemble members get to know one another and connect to the symbol of power in* Hammered.

Thor's hammer is the source of his heroic strength. Invite your cast to stand in a circle and ask them to think about from who, what, or where they gather their inner strength. Next, prompt them to select one pillar of their strength and to think of a word and gesture to represent it. Go around the circle and ask each cast member to share their name, word, and gesture with the group. After each cast member shares, the rest of the group should repeat it back to them. Repeat the process again, this time with just the person's gesture. Finally, invite actors to silently step into the center of the circle, while their castmates say their name and perform their gesture, recognizing the actor and their inner strength.

**Apply to rehearsal**: by having the actors consider from whom, what, or where their assigned characters gather their inner strength.

## SIBLING RIVALRY

*Use this to:* *explore how the dynamics of sibling rivalry can be used to create dramatic tension in storytelling.*

Remind your cast that the brotherly rivalry between Thor and Loki drives the dramatic tension throughout the play. These characters represent strength, intelligence, and talent very differently, and their different approaches sometimes challenges the other to rise to the occasion. Divide your cast into two lines facing each other and ensure that every actor has a partner, or a "sibling." Designate one line to represent Thor and the other line to represent Loki. Briefly brainstorm the strengths, qualities, and perceptions of each character. Remind your cast that Thor does not enjoy when Loki mimics what he says or does. Prompt actors who are representing Thor to begin moving from the waist up, incorporating gestures, movements, and facial expressions that they think represent his character. Instruct the Loki students to mirror Thor's movement silently, striving to perfectly match their partners' movements. Call out "Lokis lead" and encourage the pairs to switch leaders so the Thors mirror the Lokis' movements. Side coach actors throughout this activity by giving different scenarios to the group that impact their movements and relationships. (e.g., "You just discovered your sibling stole your prized possession" and "You're working together to solve a crime"). Reflect with the actors, asking them how it felt to support or lead their sibling's choices.

**Apply to rehearsal**: by having the performers who play Thor and Loki develop their physicality and relationship before rehearsing their joint scenes.

## THE LANGUAGE OF ASGARD

*Use this to: help actors understand and pronounce the language of Asgard.*

Invite your cast into a circle and share with them that Asgard is a city where honorable and brave peacekeepers live. In the play, Asgard is a heightened place where citizens speak in both a Shakespearean and contemporary dialect. In the Glossary (p. 36-37) you will find several Asgardian words. Write these on separate slips of paper along with their translations and distribute one to each actor. Prompt actors to memorize the word and its pronunciation. Next, ask the actors to walk around the space and greet each other silently with a nod. Prompt the actors to then greet each other with their word and a gesture. Layer in different intentions for their greetings such as, "You are greeting someone royal" or "You are greeting someone you haven't seen in Asgard before." Side coach actors to experiment with different walking and speaking tempos, volumes, gestures, and expressiveness based on the given intentions. Bring the activity to a stop by prompting actors to pair up and find their assigned word within the script. After they find the word, prompt them to create contemporary definitions for their words based on the context of the script. If time allows, invite everyone to share their unique definitions.

**Apply to rehearsal**: by expanding the glossary for the Asgardian language to ensure the cast's understanding during scene work and blocking.

### Post-Show Talkbacks
Post-Show Talkbacks encourage audiences to forge deeper connections with your production. The following prompts can help start the conversation:

- The characters in this play are technically gods, but they have very human strengths and weaknesses. Identify some.
- What motivates Loki to deceive his brother?

## THOR & LOKI ORIGIN SKETCH

The following sketch introduces key characters and history of Asgard as a way to promote *Hammered*. It can be performed anywhere that attracts an audience (the cafeteria, for example) or filmed and posted on the school or theater's website; it can even be played or performed pre-show in order to familiarize your audience with our heroes. Additionally, you may also consider publishing The Origin of Thor & Loki (p. V) in your program.

---

> *(**THE HERALD** enters, blatting trumpet. A lot. A coterie of **ACTORS** follows.)*

**THE HERALD.** Mortal denizens of Midgard! *(several trumpet blats)* Readers and non-readers of Marvel Comics' *The Mighty Thor*! *(a couple more blats)* I, The Royal Herald of Asgard, bid you attend this merry band as they present a brief pageant wherein we elucidate the history of Asgard and its most prominent *dramatis personae*!

> *(**VOLSTAGG** takes center stage and mimes being a tree.)*

**VOLSTAGG.** Behold! Yggdrasil! The World Tree!

> *(**THOR, LOKI**, and **SIF** do a dance around **VOLSTAGG**, making "woowoo" noises.)*

**THOR.** For time immemorial, The World Tree's cosmic branches have linked the Nine Realms of the galaxy together.

**SIF.** At the trunk of the tree sits earthly Midgard, whose ignorant mortal denizens – no offense – believe the gods of Asgard to be naught but the stuff of Norse mythology.

**LOKI.** But beyond primitive Midgard lie other realms of fire and ice and dark matter...

> *(**THOR, LOKI**, and **SIF** chant as they map out the realms on **VOLSTAGG**'s tree-body.)*

**SIF**. Svartalfheim and Jotunheim, up and up and up we climb!

**LOKI**. Nifelheim and Helheim, hey, it's time for Vanaheim!

**THOR**. Muspelheim and Alfheim... can't think of another rhyme!

**VOLSTAGG**. *(steps forward, reclaiming his dignity with his best Orson Welles)* But of all the Nine Realms, only one hangs from the top bough of the World Tree like a succulent, golden pear. Asgard! Realm of the gods!

**THOR**. For millennia, Asgard has ruled over the Nine Realms with benevolence, charity, and grace.

**SIF**. And what godly lord could possibly embody the very essence of this dominion?

**LOKI**. Odin! All Father. King. Warrior. Husband. God.

> *(**ODIN** steps forward doing his best kingly wave.)*

**ODIN**. Friends, Asgardians, countrymen, lend me your ears! Five thousand years ago, I, Odin, crested my mother Bestla's womb with a mighty yawp! In that short time, I have ruled Asgard, waged war, made peace, and married the strongest, wisest woman I've known... your queen, Freyja!

> *(**FREYJA** bows regally.)*

And yet! I am a hollow shell of a man.

**FREYJA**. I know you well, husband. Your biological clock is ticking. 'Tis the laughter of children you crave. And more, an heir to the throne of Asgard. *(breaks character to address the audience)* And so, through mysterious, complicated circumstances best explained in trade paperback collections of Marvel Comics, the King and Queen were bestowed two sons, two princely heirs.

**THOR**. Thor, God of Thunder.

**LOKI**. And Loki, God of Mischief. *(offering his brother a handshake)* Brother.

**THOR**. Broth—

(**LOKI** *dodges the shake, running his hand through his hair.*)

**THOR.** Honestly?

**LOKI.** I mean, it's in my title.

**FREYJA.** My sons, step forward. Your father wishes to bequeath you each a gift.

(**ODIN** *steps forward carrying Mjolnir.*)

**ODIN.** Thor. To you I bequeath the mighty war hammer Mjolnir. When you are of age, you shall use this hammer to call thunder and lightning down upon your foes. It will also grant you the power to fly through the very heavens with the speed of a shooting star.

**THOR.** I promise to do you proud, Father.

**ODIN.** And to you, Loki... *(searching his pockets)* I bequeath... this royal pocket lint! Good news, you're already old enough for it!

**LOKI.** I also promise to do you proud, Father. And I say that with no trace of justifiable sarcasm.

**THE HERALD.** And so go forth, Midgardians! Remember well this expurgated history of Asgard! It's all you're getting for free! For more adventures of Thor and Loki, their royal parents Odin and Freyja...

**SIF.** And the as-yet-uncredited Sif...

**VOLSTAGG.** And Volstagg...

**THE HERALD.** ... get thee to *Hammered: A Thor & Loki Play*, being performed *(INSERT SHOW DETAILS)*. Asgard awaits.

(**THE HERALD** *blats proudly off as the* **ACTORS** *follow.*)

### End of Sketch

### MUSIC USE NOTE

Licensees are solely responsible for obtaining formal written permission from copyright owners to use copyrighted music in the performance of this play and are strongly cautioned to do so. If no such permission is obtained by the licensee, then the licensee must use only original music that the licensee owns and controls. Licensees are solely responsible and liable for all music clearances and shall indemnify the copyright owners of the play(s) and their licensing agent, Concord Theatricals Corp., against any costs, expenses, losses and liabilities arising from the use of music by licensees. Please contact the appropriate music licensing authority in your territory for the rights to any incidental music.

### IMPORTANT BILLING AND CREDIT REQUIREMENTS

If you have obtained performance rights to this title, please refer to your licensing agreement for important billing and credit requirements.

CPSIA information can be obtained
at www.ICGtesting.com
Printed in the USA
BVHW040855180321
602887BV00013B/1989